Cow Goes for a Ride

New Kids Media™ is published by Baker Book House Company, P.O. Box 6287, Grand Rapids, MI 49516-6287

ISBN 0-8010-4504-5

Printed in China

1  2  3  4  5  6  7  –  05  04  03  02

# CoW
## Goes for a Ride

BAKER
A DIVISION OF
Baker Book House Co

Cow loved wandering around
the farm, chatting with her
friends about this and that.

On one particular stroll, Cow saw her friends huddled at the far end of the barn. What were they talking about? Cow edged closer.

"But I've only ever seen Farmer do that," said Chicken. "Do what?" asked Cow. "Yes, but none of us has ever even tried it!" said Goat. "Tried what?" asked Cow.

"You're right!" exclaimed Pig, "One of us really should investigate!" "Investigate what?" asked Cow. "But who will do it?" asked Chicken. "Do what?" asked Cow. Then, worried she might miss out on something, Cow exclaimed, "I'll do it!"

"You will?" asked Goat. "Great!" said Pig. "Go ahead! Then maybe we'll all try it!" Cow thought for a minute and said, "Mmmm . . . what am I doing again?"

"Why, climbing to the top of the big green tractor and sitting where Farmer sits, of course!" answered Goat. "Oh, my. I don't know if I can do that," said Cow. "Farmer told us to not play with his machines."

"Aw, c'mon!" said Chicken. "You'll be fine! Besides, you said you would do it!" "That's right . . ." the others cried. "We all heard you say you would!" Cow knew she said that. She didn't know what she was talking about, but she had said it.

"OK," Cow said. "Maybe it wouldn't hurt to climb on the big green tractor just once." With that, she began to get on the tractor. It wasn't as difficult as she had imagined. She found good parts to hold onto, and good places to stand.

"This is OK!" Cow said. "I think I'm going to make it!" The other animals watched excitedly as she reached the top of the tractor and sat down where Farmer always sat.

After a few seconds of silence, Cow exclaimed, "Wow! Come on, everyone! Climb on the back!" All the other animals crawled onto the flatbed trailor hooked behind the tractor.

Cow was having fun. She completely forgot the rule about not playing with any of the farm machines. "Look at me!" Cow mooed, "I'm Farmer!"

Cow made noises like she was driving the tractor. She turned the steering wheel back and forth, she pushed all the buttons, and she twisted all the knobs!

**ROAR!** Suddenly the tractor made an incredible noise! Everyone froze. "Uh oh," Cow thought.

Cow began to climb down, but as she turned sideways on the seat, she bumped another knob. ZOOM! The tractor lurched forward! All of the animals on the flatbed fell over and Cow fell back down into the seat. "Hold On!" hollered Pig!

Cow grabbed the steering wheel to hold on. "What do I do?!" she cried.

BOOM! Suddenly the tractor crashed through some barrels and tools that Farmer had neatly stacked in the barn. Cow turned the wheel as fast as she could and the tractor roared out of the barn and across the field.

CRASH! The tractor broke through the fence! "Oh, no!" yelled Pig as the tractor zipped across the field.

FOOMP! The tractor
exploded through a big
haystack. Hay flew
everywhere, landing all
over Cow and her
friends. "What are you
doing?" shouted Horse.

"Stop this thing!" shrieked Goat.
"I don't know how!" Cow yelled as
the tractor tore across the end of the
field. Suddenly Cow saw the pond.
They were headed right for it!

Cow twisted the steering wheel with all of her strength, but the tractor splashed into the edge of the pond! FOOSH! Cow kept turning the wheel, and the tractor roared onto the edge of the field . . .

. . . and kept roaring ahead. ZOOM! Before anyone could think about what was happening, the tractor narrowly missed a tree! The branches that had been peacefully hanging down now were klonking each animal in the head on their way past. Bonk! Bonk! Bonk! Bonk! Bonk!

Now the tractor rolled down a small bank toward the river. Oh, how Cow wished she had obeyed the rules about Farmer's machines.

SPLAT! Suddenly the tractor stopped. The wheels were still turning, but the tractor wasn't going anywhere! "What was happening?" Cow and her friends wondered.

They watched silently as the wheels soon stopped moving, too, and the tractor settled into the soft clay that lined the river. The tractor shut down and now there was only the sound of the trickling river water.

Just as each animal was thinking, "Uh oh," a familiar voice called, "What in the world has happened?!" It was Farmer! He had seen the runaway tractor and chased after it.

Cow looked at him with watery eyes. "You silly animals could have been seriously hurt!" Farmer said. "You knew you weren't supposed to play with the farm equipment, and now look what's happened!"

"If only we had followed the rules!" Cow thought. She felt so sorry. She mooed, "I know that there is a reason for rules, even when I don't understand them."

"God has given us some rules, too!" Farmer said. "Those rules must be important to have come from God." Cow knew that Farmer only wanted what was best for her. She promised to try to obey the rules. She also remembered God's rules were meant to keep us safe.

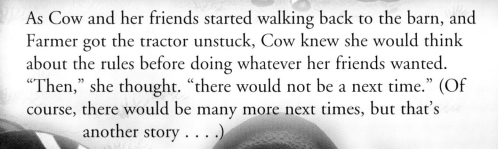

As Cow and her friends started walking back to the barn, and Farmer got the tractor unstuck, Cow knew she would think about the rules before doing whatever her friends wanted. "Then," she thought. "there would not be a next time." (Of course, there would be many more next times, but that's another story . . . .)